My Words ROAR!

By Mary DiPalermo

Illustrated by
Nina Rouselle de Polonia

Scholastic Inc.

To my mom, who taught me a lifetime of tools.
And to my darling, roaring family. I love you all.

—M.D.

Text copyright © 2018 by Mary DiPalermo.

Illustrations copyright © by Scholastic Inc.

ISBN 978-1-338-24470-0

10 9 8   20 21 22

Printed in the U.S.A.   40

First printing 2018

Book design by Lizzy Yoder

Sometimes my thoughts and feelings are wild and powerful.

ROAR!

Like big, roaring dinosaurs.   I just can't control them.

I get a thought. Then I share it. No matter where I am.

Or at the movies.

"Teddy told me how this movie ends . . .

ROAR!

the neighbor's a SPY!"

I can be in my classroom.

Or in the library.

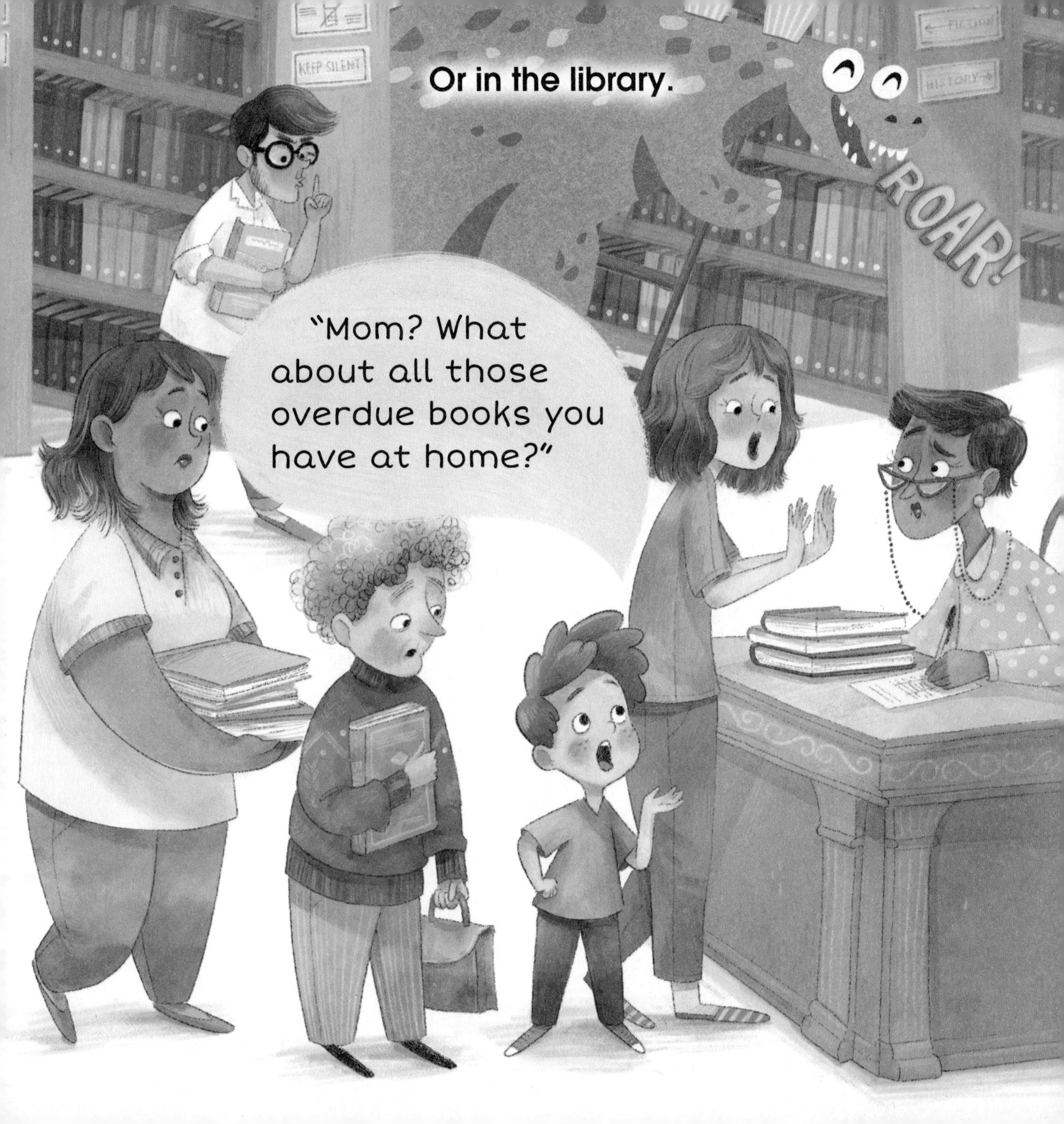

It sometimes bothers people when my thoughts come blurting out.

Or when my words interrupt their words.

So Mom and I invented a talking tool. We call it the KISS! KISS stands for *Keep It Silent Sweetie*! It helps me to stop and think *before* interrupting.

Of course, if there's an emergency—like an overflowing bathtub or a brother with a boo-boo—I speak up right away.

Keep It Silent Sweetie

But for all those *other* times, I'm learning to be respectful and wait my turn. That's good manners!

If I get a big, important thought while someone else is talking . . . or I'm in a quiet space . . .

or my thought is private . . .

I give my pointing finger a KISS, which reminds me to *Keep It Silent Sweetie!*

S S S S S

It's super silly!

5

4

The other day, I was with Grandma. She was talking to her friend about something serious.

I forgot to KISS.

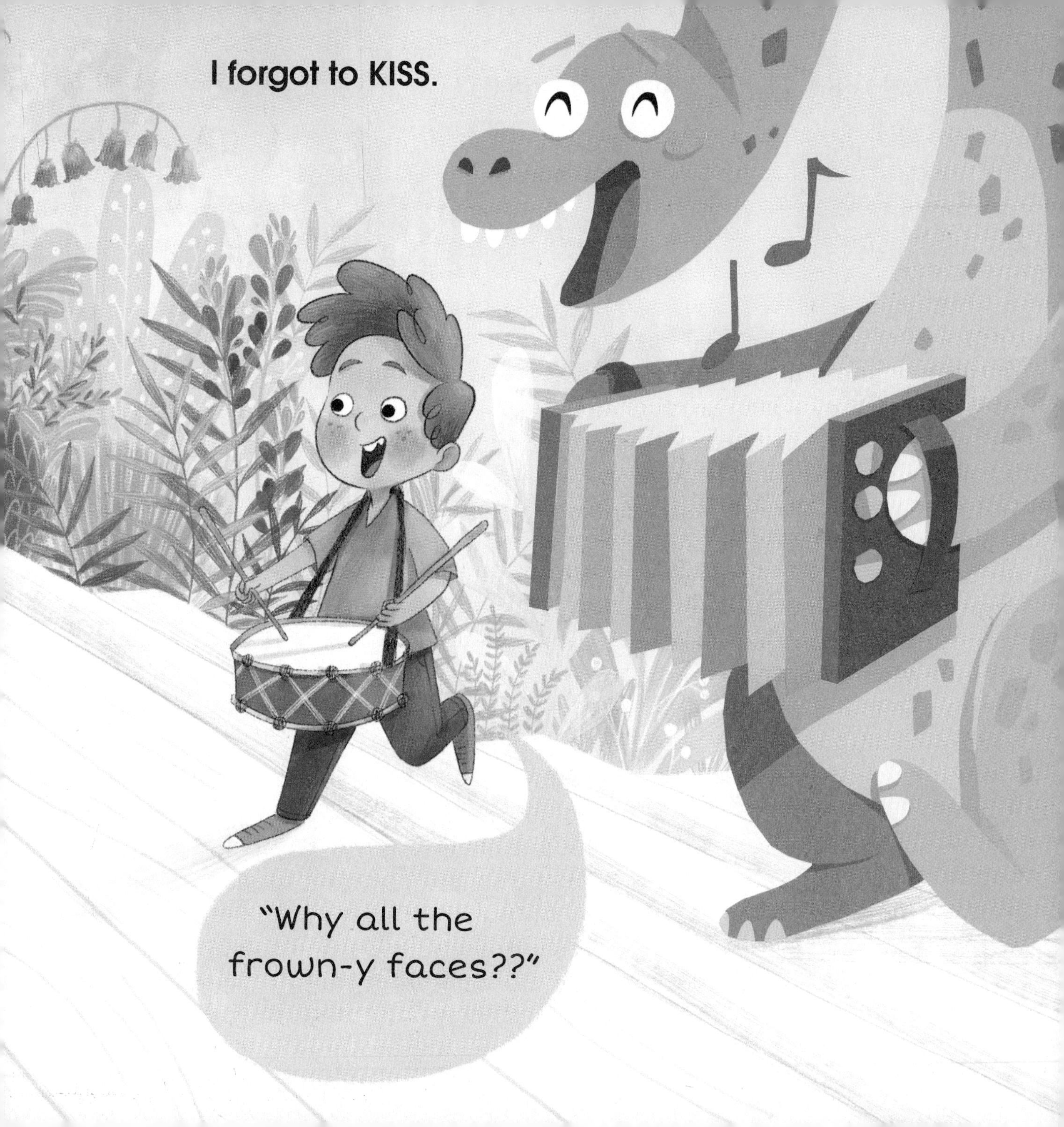

Then my friend Annabel drew a picture of her pet frog.

Grandma wasn't happy and Annabel wasn't happy, which made me unhappy, too.

I thought . . . and I thought some more. I decided to practice the KISS. And guess what? I started to remember to do it all by myself!

That evening, I didn't interrupt at dinner.

Then the next day, I waited to ask my question until story time was over.

Soon, I was seeing lots of happy faces . . .
and that made me feel happy, too!

My thoughts are *still* super powerful, like great big dinosaurs. But instead of letting them *roar*, now I just give them a KISS!

About This Book:

My Words Roar! was developed to help introduce children to the ideas of courtesy and impulse control. Parents can use this story at home to help guide social skills. Teachers can use this book at school to start group discussions about listening and waiting one's turn to speak.

Helpful Tips:

✳ Remind children that it is *always* okay to speak up when there's an emergency. Discuss the difference between interrupting versus speaking up when there's something important to share.

✳ Talk to your child about how to evaluate a situation to determine if it's a good time to share their thoughts. Talk about how words are powerful, and ask your child how they would feel if someone interrupted them.

✳ Discuss how important it is to listen. Why is it important for children to listen at home? How about at school?

✳ Create a method that works for you and your child! This book introduces the tool *Keep It Silent Sweetie*. Some other ideas include:

  ✳ Teach your child to *Stop, Look, and Listen* to see if the time is right to share their thoughts aloud. What is going on around them?

  ✳ Encourage your child to take a deep breath in and out before speaking, using the time to visualize their words going out with their breath. Do the words still seem like a good idea to share in that moment? Are these words that might be hurtful to someone else?

Our words can be powerful.
This story can help us know when best to use them.